HUCK
FINN

Retold by Pauline Francis

READZONE BOOKS

First published in 2007

British Library Cataloguing in Publication Data (CIP) is available for this title.

ISBN 978-93-5275-586-8

Cover design and illustration by Emil Dacanay, D.R.Ink
Inside illustrations by Mike Spoor

Visit our website: www.readzonebooks.com

Published by Scholastic India Pvt. Ltd. under license from Readzone Book Limited.

Reprinted : 2018, 2019 (Four Time), 2020, 2021 (Twice)

Printed in India at Sterling Graphics Pvt. Ltd., Manesar

HUCKLEBERRY FINN

Introduction

Mark Twain was born in 1835, in the American state of Missouri, which borders the great Mississippi River. His real name was Samuel Langhorne Clemens. When Samuel was only twelve years old, his father died and he left school to earn his living. After travelling around America as a printer and digging for gold, Samuel became a pilot on the steamboats which travelled up and down the Mississippi.

Then Samuel worked as a journalist and he became a famous travel writer. He decided to use the name Mark Twain. This was the call of the steamboat pilots when the depth of the water was two (twain) fathoms!

In 1876, Mark Twain wrote *The Adventures of Tom Sawyer.* Eight years later, *Huckleberry Finn* was published. This book tells the adventures of Tom's friend, Huck. Huck runs away and travels down the Mississippi River on a raft with a runaway slave called Jim.

Mark Twain became famous all over the world. He died in 1910, at the age of seventy-five.

The story of *Huckleberry Finn* was set at a time (the 1850s) when slaves, were bought and sold in some American states. Many tried to escape to states where slavery was not allowed. It was a crime to help a runaway slave.

Twain uses some Missouri African-American words in the story, and other words you may not know. These are the ones I have used:

bin	been
'cos	because
dah	there
dat	that
de	the
dey	they
doan	don't
en	and
git	get
(h)ain't	hasn't/ haven't
injun	Indian
kin	can
mars	master
ole	old
pap	father
run	travel, sail
skiff	a small, light boat
warn't	wasn't
wuz	was

Some of the characters in the book also use double negatives! So '*I hain't done nuffin'* means 'I haven't done anything' and '*I hain't got no money'* means 'I haven't got any money'.

"Huckleberry Finn, son of the town drunkard, was hated and dreaded by all the mothers because he was idle, lawless, vulgar and bad – and because all the children wished they dared be like him."

The Adventures of Tom Sawyer

Chapter One

Escape!

My name is Huckleberry Finn. I live by the great Mississippi River where I have had many adventures with my friend, Tom Sawyer. Our last adventure made us rich by six thousand dollars when we tracked down a gang of robbers. Judge Thatcher kept my money safe for me and the widow Miss Douglas and her sister Miss Watson took me to live with them 'cos they thought my father was dead. They wanted to civilise me. They gave me smart clothes and read the Bible to me, but I missed the woods where I used to live. That summer, I ran away.

Tom Sawyer found me and said I could join his gang if I came back. So I did. He called for me one night and we crept past the widow's slave, Jim, sleeping by the kitchen door. In a cave in the hillside, we all swore to keep our gang a secret and we signed our names in blood. But we only met for about a month before we got bored – and we all resigned.

Come autumn, I had to go to school anyways and soon I could spell and read and write a little. At first, I hated school and played truant. Then they beat me and this cheered me up 'cos I liked being bad. I got used to living in a house, too, although sometimes I climbed out of the window and slept in the woods. Miss Watson said if I behaved, I would go to a good place when I died.

'Will Tom Sawyer go there?' I asked her.

She shook her head. So I decided not to try to get there, because I wanted him and me to be together.

One morning, well into winter, I knocked over the salt

on the table. When I reached out to throw some over my shoulder, to keep off bad luck, Miss Watson stopped me. I set off for school feeling worried and shaky. Then I saw the tracks in the snow – a cross in the left boot-heel made with big nails to keep off the devil. My pap's boot! I ran down the hill to Judge Thatcher's house and I made him swap all my money for just one dollar.

That night, when I lit the candle and went up to my room, there sat my pap. He had climbed in through the window. I used to be scared of him because he beat me. But now he just looked old.

'I hear you're high-and-mighty now,' he said. 'I come to git the money. I want it. *Now*!'

'I hain't got no money, pap,' I told him. 'Only a dollar.'

He took my dollar, went into town and got drunk.

My pap caused nothing but trouble until the spring. He thrashed me for going to school and he took Judge Thatcher to court to try to get back my money. Then he took me across the river to the Illinois side to live in a log hut. During the day, we fished and hunted with his gun. At night, he locked the door and put the key under his head when he slept. As my pap got drunker and drunker, he started to beat me. I couldn't stand it.

'I've *got* to escape!' I thought.

I found an old saw in the roof and cut a hole in the wall behind the bed and waited for my chance. In June, the river began to rise as it always did. When pap sent me out fishing, I stood on the bank and looked at all the rubbish in the water. Along came an old canoe and I paddled it ashore.

That's when I had the idea. That night, when pap locked me in and went out drinking, I crawled out through the hole. I loaded the canoe with corn, coffee and bacon, a fishing line, blankets – and my pap's gun. Then I shot a wild pig. I cut its throat in the cabin and let it bleed everywhere. I filled a sack with stones and dragged it – and the pig - to the river where they sank to the bottom. Then I pulled out some of my hair and stuck it onto an axe.

It was near dark now. I sat in the canoe under some willow trees and smoked my pipe.

'They'll follow the track of that sack of rocks to the river,' I thought. 'Then they'll drag the river for me – and hunt the robbers that killed me.' I smiled. 'They'll soon get tired of that. Then nobody'll bother about me no more!'

I decided to head for Jackson's Island.

'I know it,' I thought, 'and nobody goes there.'

I paddled down river for about two miles. Then I lay in the bottom of the canoe and smoked my pipe. The sky looks deep when you lay on your back in the moonshine.

The canoe drifted on and Jackson's Island rose up before me – big and dark, like a steamboat without any lights. I landed on the side facing the Illinois bank and fell asleep until the boom of a cannon gun from a boat woke me up.

'They're trying to make my body float to the surface,' I thought.

I watched that ferry boat all morning. It came so close that I could see them all: Pap, Judge Thatcher, Tom Sawyer and plenty more. Everybody was talking about my murder. By evening, they'd gone home.

When it was dark, I lit a camp fire, smoked my pipe and counted the stars. I was happy, but lonesome. The next day, I started to explore the island and collected grapes and strawberries and green raspberries.

But on the fourth day, I came across the warm ashes of a camp fire. Somebody else was on the island!

Chapter Two

A runaway slave

My heart pounded as I tip-toed away from that fire. When I reached my camp, I climbed into a tree until dark. Then I thought, 'I'm going to find out who it is.'

So I took my paddle and slid out from the shore. The moon made it as light as day. I went to the same place and, sure enough, I glimpsed a fire through the trees. A man was sitting next to it.

It was Miss Watson's slave, Jim.

'Hello, Jim!' I cried.

Jim knelt down to pray. 'Doan hurt ole Jim!' he cried. 'You go en git in de river again where you belongs.'

'I ain't dead, Jim!' I said.

As we cooked up breakfast, I told him what I had done. I knew he wouldn't tell anybody.

'What are *you* doing here, Jim?' I asked.

'I…I run off,' he said. 'One night, I hear the slave trader talkin' to Ole Missus Watson. He says she can git eight hundred dollars for me. De dogs track me if I go on foot. So I git a raft I see en de river.'

Jim said there was rain on the way because the birds were settling in the trees. He knew all the bad luck signs.

'Ain't there no good luck signs, Jim?' I asked.

'A few,' he said, 'en dey ain't no use to nobody.'

We put all our things in a cave in a steep hillside. Then we hid the canoe in the willow trees. The river rose and rose for twelve days until it was over the river banks and the low parts of the island.

One morning, at dawn, a house came floating by, with

a dead man inside. But Jim wouldn't let me go close to look at him. He said it would bring bad luck. We took all the clothes we could find and an old straw hat – and eight dollars sewn into an old overcoat.

Well, the days went along after that and the water slowly went down.

'I'm gettin' bored, Jim,' I said. 'I need an adventure. I'm goin' over to the shore.'

It was Jim who suggested that I dress in the girl's clothes we had taken from the floating house. I put on a gown over my rolled up trousers, practised my walking and set off for the Illinois bank at dusk. In a little wooden hut, I saw a woman knitting by the candlelight. I knocked at the door.

'Come in,' the woman said. 'What's your name, honey?'

'Sarah Williams,' I told her.

She chattered on. 'Poor Huck Finn's been murdered. People around here think that slave Jim did it. He ran off that very same night. There's reward for him – three hundred dollars.'

'Are they after him then?' I asked.

'Yes, child,' she replied. 'I seen smoke on Jackson's Island. He's hiding there, I bet you. My husband's going over there at midnight.' She stared at me. 'What did you say your name was, honey?'

'Er…M…Mary Williams,' I said.

'I thought you said it was Sarah, honey.'

'Oh, yes, ma'am,' I said quickly. 'Sarah Mary Williams.'

'Come, now, what's your real name?' she asked. 'Bill, Tom or…?'

I shook like a leaf. 'George Peters, ma'am,' I mumbled.

'Don't be afraid, honey,' she said. 'Tell me what

happened.'

I told her how my parents were dead and how I had to work for an old farmer who beat me and how I had run away to find my uncle. She listened kindly. Then she gave me some food and said, 'Now get along to your uncle, Sarah Mary Williams George Peters.'

I slipped into the night. The town clock struck eleven as I reached the island. I ran to the cave and roused Jim.

'There ain't a minute to lose, Jim!' I cried. 'They're after us!'

It must have been one o'clock by the time we were well beyond the island with the raft and the canoe. Nobody followed us. At dawn, we tied up on a sand bar thick with cotton bushes and lay there all day, watching the rafts and steamboats moving along the Mississippi. Jim made a wigwam with a raised floor on the raft. That night, we set off again. We hung a lantern when we saw a steamboat coming down, to keep us from getting run over.

With the help of the current, we travelled at about four miles an hour. We talked and caught fish and sometimes took a swim. Every night, I sneaked ashore to some little village to buy flour and bacon or other stuff to eat. Once, I stole a chicken. And another time, I slipped into the cornfields and borrowed a melon or a pumpkin.

'It's not wrong to borrow,' Pap used to say, 'so long as you mean to pay them back.'

'Borrowing's just another name for stealing,' the widow Douglas used to say.

On the fifth night we passed the town of St Louis. And a few days down river from there, a huge storm broke out just after midnight. When the lightning flashed, we saw a steamboat wrecked on the rocks.

'Let's land on her, Jim,' I said.

Jim shook his head.

'We might borrow something worth having,' I said. 'Steamboat captains is always rich. Come on, Jim! Do you reckon Tom Sawyer would let an adventure like this go by? I wish *he* was here.'

Jim grumbled, but he gave in. Soon we were sneaking around on board – and hearing quarrelling voices. In the captain's cabin, we glimpsed a man tied up on the floor with two men standing over him.

'Quick, Jim!' I whispered into the darkness. 'Get the raft and set their skiff loose as well!'

A few minutes later, Jim whispered back, 'Oh, my lordy, lordy! Dah ain't no raft, Huck! She broke loose en gone!'

Chapter Three

The accident

I almost fainted. 'We're shut up here with a gang of murderers!' I thought. 'We've got to get *their* skiff for ourselves!'

We found their skiff just in time. I cut the rope and away we went. We didn't use the oars or speak or hardly breathe. But we glided swiftly until the steamboat disappeared into the night. Then, in the pouring rain, Jim rowed hard as we looked for our raft. When it floated past us, we jumped aboard.

'Carry on downstream for about two miles, Jim!' I shouted. 'Then light the lantern and wait for me. Those murderers shall hang for what they've done.'

I rowed their skiff to the shore, alongside a ferryboat. I wept as I told the watchman my story: how my pap and mam and sis were stranded on the wrecked steamboat.

'Please, *please* rescue them, sir!' I begged.

As soon as he'd gone to get more help, I pushed out into the river. And by the time I spotted Jim's light, the sky was beginning to get light. We made for an island, hid the raft, sank the skiff and slept the sleep of the dead.

'Three more nights and we'll be at Cairo,' I told Jim the next morning. 'That's where the Ohio River flows in. We'll go up the Ohio, Jim, to a free state, where there ain't no slavery.'

On the second night, a thick fog came down. I paddled ahead in the canoe to tie us to a sand bank; but the current was so strong that it carried the raft away. I paddled after it into the thick white fog.

A whooping cry came from my left, to my right – then from behind me. I kept answering it and paddling. My heart was thumping. For half an hour, I whooped and followed the answering cry. At last, the fog disappeared and the stars came out. In the distance, I saw the black speck of the raft. When I reached it, Jim was asleep.

'Is dat you, Huck?' he asked, opening his eyes. 'Where you bin, whooping in dat fog?'

I told Jim that I had been there all night, that there had been no fog, no whooping noises. 'You bin dreamin', Jim,' I said.

He looked at me sadly. 'I's so thankful you ain't drowned, Huck,' he said, 'so how comes you make a fool of ole Jim?'

I was so ashamed of myself that I told him the truth. And I never played a mean trick on him again.

We started out again that night, drifting round a big bend edged with thick woods. Jim sat watching for the Ohio River where he would be a free man.

'What will Miss Watson think o' me?' I thought. 'I've helped her slave to freedom when she's treated me well.'

Suddenly, Jim leapt to his feet. 'Dat's de good ole Cairo over there!' he shouted. 'We're safe, Huck!'

'I'll take the canoe and go and see,' I said.

I shoved off. Fifty yards off the shore, along came a skiff with two men in it, carrying guns. I asked them if we'd come to Cairo, but they wouldn't tell me.

'Is that your raft?' they asked. 'Are there men on it?'

'Just one man, sir,' I replied.

'Is he black or white?' they asked.

'He's white,' I said. 'It's my pap up there, and he's sick.'

'What's the matter with him, boy?'

'It's the…well, it ain't much,' I began. 'I…'

''Your papa's got the smallpox, ain't he?' they said angrily. 'Don't try to land. Here, take this.' They handed me forty dollars. 'Goodbye, boy!' they shouted. 'And if you see any runaway slaves, get them and you can make more money.'

Jim was hiding in the water when I got back to the raft. He climbed aboard. 'You save ole Jim, Huck!' he cried, 'and I ain't going' to forgit you for dat, honey.'

'But I still ain't no idea where Cairo is,' I said.

We ran for two more days without reaching Cairo. Soon we realised that we must have passed it in the fog.

'We can't take the raft upstream,' I said. 'The current's too strong. We'll have to take the canoe back up there tonight.'

We slept in the cotton bushes all day. But when we went back to the river at dusk, the canoe had gone. We decided to carry on downstream and buy another canoe at the next ferry stop.

A thick fog came down again and we heard a steamboat coming along the river: voices yelling, bells ringing and steam hissing. We quickly hung up our lantern, but it was too late!

As the steamboat crashed into us, Jim and I jumped into the muddy water of the great Mississippi.

Chapter Four

Ambush

I dived deep to let that thirty foot steamboat wheel go over me. Then I called out, 'Jim! Jim!' a dozen times, but there was no reply. I grabbed a plank of wood and struck out for the shore without him. As soon as I got there, a pack of dogs jumped out on me outside a log cabin.

'Who's there?' a man's voice shouted. 'Are you a Shepherdson?'

'No, I'm George Jackson!' I replied. 'I only want to walk by, but the dogs won't let me.'

'What are you prowling around for at this time o' the night, hey?' the man asked.

'I warn't prowling, sir,' I said. 'I fell overboard from the steamboat.'

I heard people stirring inside the house. They unbolted the door and I went in. Three big men pointed guns at me. An old woman and two young women stood behind them. The Grangerfords – for that was their name – gave me dry clothes and corn-beef and buttermilk to drink. I shared a room with Buck, one of their sons. The family owned a lot of farms and over a hundred black slaves – and they were always quarrelling with their rich neighbours, the Shepherdsons.

One day, Jack, one of the family slaves, told me to walk with him down to the swamps. Curious, I followed him for about a mile. We walked through some trees – and there was Jim, hidden in the tangled vines.

He wasn't surprised to see me alive because he'd swum behind me that night. But he didn't shout to me 'cos he didn't want nobody to pick him up and take him into slavery again.

'Why didn't you fetch me sooner?' I asked him.

'I was patchin' up de raft,' he said. 'She's as good as new agin, Huck!'

I don't want to say much about what happened the next day. When I woke up that morning, Buck had gone and the house was quiet.

'Mars Buck's sis run off in de night,' Jack told me, 'to git married to dat young Shepherdson. Ole mars and de boys rode off to kill dat young man.'

As I ran up the river road, I heard gunshots in the distance. Hiding in a tree, I saw Buck and his cousin, Joe. I called out, to warn him there were men ahead.

'My pap and my brothers are dead!' Buck cried. 'Them Shepherdsons ambushed them.'

Suddenly, a *bang! bang! bang*! came from behind them. Buck and Joe ran to the river, wounded, and swam downstream. I stayed in that tree until dark. When I came down to the river, I found Buck and Joe both dead. I cried for Buck 'cos he was always kind to me. Then I paddled out to the raft and screamed for Jim to push off.

I could hardly breathe until we were out in the middle of the Mississippi. We talked and ate and smoked our pipes.

There ain't no home like a raft, we decided.

Two or three nights went by. The river was big down there, almost a mile and a half wide. We ran by night, letting the current take us along. We wore few clothes, unless the mosquitoes were bad. Sometimes, we had the whole river to ourselves, except for a steamboat or two. When day broke, we tied up in the cotton bushes and set up our fishing lines. After cooking up a hot breakfast, we slept.

One morning, I borrowed a canoe and paddled up a creek to look for berries. Suddenly, two men came running towards me.

'I'm a goner now!' I thought.

But the men begged me to save them from the men and dogs chasing them.

'Run through the water, that'll throw the dogs off the scent,' I said. 'Then wade down to me and get in.'

As soon as they were aboard, I made for the raft.

One of the men was about seventy, bald with grey whiskers. The other was about thirty. They both carried cloth bags – and they didn't know each other. They had been run out of town for selling medicines and a tooth-cleaning cream which took off all the enamel.

'*I* am a duke by birth,' the young man said.

'And *I* am the rightful king of France,' the old man said.

I knew better. They were just a couple of scoundrels. But I'd learned one thing from my pap: with men like that, you just let them get on with what they wanted. And they wanted to come with *us*.

Chapter Five

The king and the duke

The king and the duke fired questions at us. Why did we only run at night? Was Jim a runaway slave?

'A runaway slave wouldn't be heading this far south,' I said. 'Jim's *my* slave. We was going with my pap and my brother to my uncle when a steamboat struck the raft. My pap and brother drowned. People keep trying to take Jim from me, so we don't run in by day no more.'

'I'll try and think of a way to keep people off your back,' the duke said.

We left at dark. Soon it began to rain. I'd never seen such a storm. The waves almost washed me off the raft. At daybreak, we slid into the willow trees to hide. I watched the duke take out leaflets from his bag and I saw the words *Shakespeare* and *tragedy* and *theatre*.

'What do you say, king,' he said. 'The first good town we come to, we'll hire a hall and do the balcony scene in *Romeo and Juliet*?'

'I don't know much about play-acting,' the king replied. 'Can you learn me?'

'I usually play Romeo,' the duke said. 'You'll have to be Juliet.'

'What about my white whiskers?' the king asked.

'These country folk won't notice,' the duke replied.

About three miles down the bend in the river, we left Jim hiding and went into a town. While the duke went to a printing office, the king and I found our way to a preacher's meeting in the woods. There must have been a thousand people there.

You couldn't hear what the preacher man was saying, there was so much crying and shouting. Suddenly, the king ran up onto the platform beside the preacher. He told them how he had been a pirate for thirty years and now he wanted to head back to the Indian Ocean to help the pirates and turn them back to better ways.

'Only I ain't got no money!' he cried, bursting into tears.

'Take up a collection for him!' somebody shouted.

So the king went through the crowd with a hat, and he collected almost eighty-eight dollars!

When the duke came back to the raft, he was pretty pleased with himself, too. He handed us a leaflet, which said:

Runaway slave: $200 reward
He ran away from a plantation near
New Orleans last winter

'Now we can run by day,' he said. 'We'll tie Jim up, lay him in the wigwam. And if anybody asks, we'll just show 'em the notice.'

We started to run on the river after the sun was up. It was busy on the raft, with the king learning how to act and swordfight and learning his lines. When we came to the next town, the duke and the king stuck up their leaflets:

The Balcony Scene In Romeo and Juliet!!!
25 cents; children and servants, 10 cents

But there was only twelve people at the show and they only got enough to pay their expenses.

So the duke printed another leaflet, which said: **THE KING WITHOUT EQUAL – 50 cents: No ladies or**

children

That night, the hired room was full of men. When the curtain went up, the king came onto the stage, running around on all fours, his body painted in stripes like a rainbow. Everybody laughed and clapped until the curtain came down – and stayed down.

'Is that *all*?' the audience cried angrily.

'Yes,' said the duke.

A man leapt onto the stage. 'They've made a fool of us!' he cried. 'But we won't be the only laughing-stock! We'll tell everybody they've *got* to come.'

And in this way, those scoundrels got a good audience the next night. But on the third night, people pelted him with rotten eggs and vegetables.

'Run for the raft!' the king whispered to me.

In no time at all, we was gliding down the river. Ten miles below that town, we lit our pipes – and the duke and king laughed until their bones ached. They had taken four hundred and sixty-five dollars.

Chapter Six

A useful funeral

The next day, we tied up under a willow on a sand bank. There was a small town on each side of the river. The duke and the king wanted to go ashore, but Jim was tired of being tied up all day.

The duke had an idea. He dressed Jim up as a Shakespearian king – King Lear: long white robes, long white hair and a long white beard. Then he took his theatre make-up and painted Jim's face, neck and hands blue, like a man that has been drowned for nine days. He wrote a sign in the shingle: **MAD – but harmless.**

That way, Jim could move about. And if anyone came near, he had only to start screaming and shouting.

I paddled us close to the shore. Half a mile from the town, we saw a young man carrying two heavy bags. He said his name was Tim Collins and he was on his way to catch the steamboat.

'Git aboard,' the king said. 'We'll take you.'

'When I first see you,' the young man said, 'I thought you was Mr Harvey Wilks coming from England. But you can't be, 'cos you're too late.'

'No, my name's the Reverend Blodgett,' the king replied. 'I hope Mr Wilks hasn't missed anything important.'

'He's missed seeing his poor brother die,' said Tim Collins. 'Poor old Peter Wilks! He's left a letter for Harvey, telling him to make sure his three nieces get his money. He was coming with another brother, William, but he's deaf and dumb.'

'When's the funeral?' the king asked.

'Tomorrow,' he replied, 'about midday.'

When the steamboat had left, we set off for the town where Peter Wilks lived. When we arrived, the king wept and said he was the dead man's brother. The news was all over town in two minutes. Pretty soon, we were in the middle of a crowd of people who took us to Peter Wilks' house. There we found his three nieces: Mary Jane, who was beautiful and nineteen, Susan, who was fifteen, and poor Joanna who was fourteen and had a hare-lip.

The king and the duke walked slowly over to the coffin set up in the parlour. Then they put their arms around each other and cried. Everybody broke down too. Then Mary Jane fetched the letter her uncle had written: to his nieces he left his house and three thousand dollars. To his brothers, Harvey and William, he left his business and three thousand dollars each in gold.

I went with them to the cellar to fetch the money.

'I've got an idea!' the duke said, 'Let's give this money to the girls.'

'Dazzling idea!' the king agreed. 'Then they'll *all* trust us!'

When we were back upstairs, I could see the king getting ready to make another fine speech.

'Friends,' he began, 'my poor brother has been kind to these poor little lambs. What kind o' uncles would we be to rob – yes, *rob* – such poor sweet lambs. Here, Mary Jane, Susan, Joanna, take the money. Take it all as a gift.'

I've never seen such hugging and kissing. Everybody shook the hands of those frauds – until the doctor turned up at the house.

'*You*, Peter Wilks' brother!' he shouted. 'You're not an Englishman! You're a fraud, that's what you are!' He turned to the girls. 'Turn your backs on these scoundrels, I beg you!'

'Here's your answer,' Mary Jane said. She picked up the bag of gold and gave it to the king. 'Take this six thousand dollars and invest for me and my sisters.' Then she hugged him.

'You're going to feel sick when you think of this day,' the doctor said angrily.

'Then we'll send for you!' the king said.

And everybody laughed.

The girls invited us stay that night. They was so kind that I made up my mind.

'I'll git that money back for them,' I thought. 'I can't tell anybody or it'll be bad for me. I'll steal it.'

That night, I watched the duke and the king hide the money under their straw mattress. I took it when they were downstairs. As I crept outside to bury the bag, I heard a noise on the stairs. I ran into the parlour and threw the bag inside the coffin. Before dawn, I went down to the parlour, but the door was locked. And just before midday, the coffin lid was screwed down.

That's how they came to bury Mr Wilks with his own money.

Chapter Seven

Digging for gold

The next morning, I heard Mary Jane crying. She told me that the king had already sold some of the slaves because he was putting the business up for sale that day. But worse than that, the children had been sold separately from their parents.

'They'll never see one other again,' she sobbed.

'Yes, they will!' I said, without thinking.

She threw her arms around my neck. 'What do you mean, Huck?'

I bolted the door. 'I want to tell you the truth, Miss Mary. Your uncles, they ain't your uncles. Them slaves ain't his to sell, nor the business. They'll both come back to you.'

Her eyes blazed with anger as I told her everything. 'Come on!' she said. 'We'll have them tarred and feathered and flung in the river!'

'Now, listen, Miss Mary,' I said. 'I need some time to git away. If I don't turn up by eleven tonight, it means I'm safe. Then you spread the news and get those scoundrels jailed.'

'What if they leave before then?' she asked.

'They won't, I said. 'They'll have to wait for the money from the sale.' I paused. 'There's one more thing, Mary Jane. That bag o' money. They hain't got it.'

'Who got it, Huck?' she asked.

'I had it,' I said. 'I stole it to give it back to you. But I can't tell you where I hid it. I'll write it down so you can read it later.'

Mary Jane shook my hand and said she would pray for me. Then she was gone.

As the sale was taking place that afternoon, a steamboat stopped at the ferry landing. An old gentleman came into town with a younger man, who had his arm in a sling.

'I am Harvey Wilks, Peter Wilks's brother,' the old man said in a fine English voice, 'and this is his brother William.'

The king didn't turn a hair. He laughed – and so did everybody else, except for the doctor, and two men who had got off the steamer with the old man. One was the lawyer, Levi Bell. The other, a big man called Hines, came up to the king.

'I see you this mornin' in a canoe,' he said. 'You was with Tim Collins.' He looked at me. 'And *him*!'

'You said you came in on the steamer!' somebody shouted.

'You're a fraud and a liar!' Hines cried.

'Neighbours!' the doctor said. 'Let's go and sort this out in the tavern.'

We all gathered in a big room and lit the candles. The doctor spoke first. 'If these men…,' He looked at us… 'ain't frauds, they won't mind showing us the bag o' money, ain't that so?'

The king pulled a sad face. 'Gentlemen, I wish I had it,' he said, 'but, alas, it ain't there. I hid it inside the straw mattress and the slaves I just sold stole it.'

The doctor asked me if I came from England, too. I nodded and started to talk about England, until the lawyer laughed and told me to sit down.

'I reckon you ain't used to lying, boy,' he said.

Levi Bell asked the king and the old gentleman to write a sentence on a piece of paper. Then he took some of Peter

Wilks's letters from his pocket and compared them.

'*None* of you wrote these letters!' he cried.

'Now, listen.' The old gentleman said. 'My brother writes all my letters for me. That's his handwriting in your letters.'

'Get him to write a line or two, then,' he said.

'He can't write with a broken arm,' the old gentleman replied. 'But I've thought of something else. Who helped to get my brother ready for burying?'

Two men put up their hands. The old gentleman turned towards the king. 'What was tattooed on his chest?' he asked.

The king turned pale. 'That's a tough question, ain't it? Yes, sir, I can tell you. A small thin blue arrow and if you don't look close, you can't see it.'

The two men shook their heads.

'What you can see is a small P and a B and a W,' the old gentleman said.

The two men shook their heads. The crowd shouted, 'They're *all* frauds!'

Levi Bell jumped onto the table. 'Gentlemen!' he shouted back. 'Listen! There's one way to prove this! Let's go and dig up the body.'

I was scared then. They marched us to the graveyard, a mile down the river. The whole town came out, too, for we made such noise. Lightning flashed and the wind began to shiver in the trees. The men dug and dug until they pulled out the coffin and took off the lid.

Suddenly, a flash of lightning lit up the coffin.

'By jingo, here's a bag of gold lying across his chest!' somebody called out.

Hines, who was holding me, whooped and let go of my wrist. I ran and ran, back through the empty town. Then I borrowed a canoe to take me out to the raft.

'Come on, Jim!' I shouted. 'Untie her. We're free of those frauds at last!'

But with the next flash of lightning, I saw the king and the duke coming over the water towards us in a skiff. When he got aboard, the king grabbed me by the collar and shook me hard.

'Tired of our company, hey?' he shouted.

But another chance came a few days later. I paddled the king and the duke into a town further down the river. I left them there and rushed back to the raft.

'Set her loose, Jim!' I shouted. 'We're leaving!'

But there was no answer. Jim had gone!

Chapter Eight

An old friend

I ran this way and that in the woods, shouting, but it warn't no use. Then I sat down and cried. But I couldn't stay still for long. I walked along the road until I met a boy. I described Jim to him.

'Yeh, I seen him at Silas Phelp's place,' he said. 'He's got a saw mill about two miles down the river. He's a runaway slave, ain't he? There's a two hundred dollar reward on him.'

'Who told on him?' I asked.

'An old fellow – a stranger,' the boy said. 'He sold him for forty dollars 'cos he couldn't wait around here no more.'

'The king!' I thought to myself. 'After all we done for him, he's made Jim a slave agin, and all for forty dollars!'

I decided to write to Miss Watson. It would be better for Jim to be a slave at home with his family if he *had* to be a slave.

"***Miss Watson,"*** I wrote, "***Your runaway slave Jim is down here two miles below Picksville. Mr Phelps has got him and he will give him up for the reward if you send it.*** HUCK FINN"

Then I thought, 'She might be so cross that she'll just sell him again.'

'And what about *me*?' I asked myself. 'The whole town would know I'd helped a runaway slave!'

I tore up the letter. I felt so wicked that I knelt down in the wigwam and tried to pray, but the words didn't come.

At last, I decided. *I* would free Jim again.

The next morning, I hid the raft out at a wooded island and took the canoe to Phelp's sawmill. It was all quiet and still and hot, but the dogs heard me coming. Fifteen of them circled me, barking, until a woman came out from the house, followed by her children. She ran over to me, smiling.

'It's *you*, at last!' she said. '*Ain't* it!'

I said, 'Yes, ma'am,' before I could stop myself.

She hugged me tight. 'Don't call me ma'am, I'm your Aunt Sally. I'm so glad to see you, dear.' She turned to the children. 'Look, it's your cousin, Tom,' she cried. 'Come on, Tom! Tell me everything! How's my dear sister Polly?'

'I'll have to tell her the truth,' I thought.

As I opened my mouth to speak, my aunt pushed me behind her. An old gentleman was coming through the gate.

'Has Tom come on the steamboat, Silas?' Aunt Sally asked, trying not to laugh.

'No,' the man replied sadly, 'and I'm worried. Where *is* he?'

'What will my sister Polly say!' she said. Then she pulled me out in front of him, laughing.

'Who's this?' the man asked.

'Why, it's our nephew, Tom Sawyer!' she replied.

I almost fell over. I was so glad to find out who I was. I told Aunt Sally and Uncle Silas all the news about the Sawyer family. Being my friend Tom was easy and comfortable.

'But what will happen when Tom turns up?' I thought.

So I told them I had to fetch my baggage from the ferry landing. They let me take their horse and wagon. And half-way there, I met Tom Sawyer, coming from the steamboat.

'I hain't done you no harm, Huck,' he gasped. 'Why have you come back to haunt me?'

'I hain't come back, Tom,' I said. 'I hain't dead.'

'Honest injun, you ain't no ghost?' he asked.

'Honest injun, I ain't,' I replied.

I told him everything. And when I told him what had happened to Jim, he thought long and hard.

'I'll *help* you steal him back, Huck,' he said.

Tom told Aunt Sally that he was his younger brother, Sid and he was given a warm welcome. That night, at supper, Uncle Silas told us there was a show on in town. The runaway slave had told him about it.

As soon as we was sent to bed, we climbed out of the bedroom window, slipped down the lightning rod and headed for town. There we ran into a crowd of people, shouting and yelling and pulling along the duke and the king.

They were covered in tar and feathers.

In spite of what they had done, I was sorry. It was a terrible thing to see. Human beings can be very cruel to one another.

Chapter Nine

Tom's plan

When we got back to the house, everybody was asleep.

'I bet I know where they're keeping Jim,' Tom said. 'When we was eating dinner, I saw one of the slaves take some food out to that little cabin down by the fence. Now, you think of a plan to set him free, Huck, and I'll think o' one. Then we'll choose the best.'

I went on thinking, but I knew whose plan it would be.

'Ready?' Tom asked.

I nodded. 'I'll bring up the canoe and fetch the raft,' I said. 'We'll steal the key to the hut and head off down the river at night, the way Jim and me used to.'

'That's too simple!' Tom said. 'It's as mild as goose milk! Now listen to mine!'

First of all, Tom said we had to know if it *was* Jim down there in that cabin. We was up at dawn the next day to make friends with the slave that took the food to Jim.

'Is that food for the dog?' Tom asked him.

'Yes, Mars Sid,' the man replied, 'and a strange kind o' dog. Does you want to go en look at 'im? There's witches in the dark. I doan like goin' there alone.'

So we went along – and it was Jim sitting there and he just had time to squeeze my hand.

Back in our room, Tom started to complain. 'This whole thing's just too easy, Huck. In the books, they have watchmen and dogs to drug... and rope ladders made from sheets... and a shirt...'

'What does Jim want a shirt for?' I asked.

'To write his diary on,' Tom said. 'And he'll need a pen

and ink…unless he uses his own blood. Borrow a sheet and shirt, Huck, and a candlestick…'

'What for?' I interrupted again.

'We'll cut it up for pens,' he said. 'And we wants knives.'

'*Knives*, Tom?'

'They always digs with knives in the books,' he said. 'That Frenchman who dug his way out of that castle on the rocks, it took him thirty seven year – and he came out in China.'

'Jim don't know nobody in China, Tom,' I said.

'Neither did the Frenchman,' Tom replied.

'Anyways, Jim won't last thirty-seven years,' I said.

That night, we climbed through the window and slid down the lightning rod. We dug 'til midnight, 'til our hands were blistered. So I got a shovel and we soon dug a good hole under the cabin and crawled up right under Jim's bed. He was glad to see us and he cried and called us honey.

His leg was chained to the leg of the bed.

'We'll saw that in two, and smuggle in a rope-ladder,' Tom whispered to him. 'And a shirt and a pen.'

Jim couldn't see much sense in it, I knew that, but he just nodded. We smoked a pipe together and Tom and I went home to bed in high spirits.

'It's the most fun I ever had,' he said. 'Now we got to bake the pie.'

'*Pie,* Tom? What for?'

'Why, to hide the rope-ladder in, Huck!' he explained. 'They do that in books!'

There was trouble when Aunt Sally discovered a candlestick, and candles and a shirt and sheet were missing. She counted them over and over again until she grew red-faced and angry. But we had troubles of our own. The sheet wouldn't fit in the pie. So we tore off a strip and threw away the rest.

Tom didn't stop at that. Prisons in books had rocks for prisoners to scratch their names on, he said, and spiders and rats and snakes. He found a grindstone in the bushes and dragged it through the hole into the cabin. And he filled the cabin with spiders and rats and snakes.

By the end of three weeks, everything was in pretty good shape. The shirt had been taken in, and every time a rat bit Jim he got up and wrote in his diary, words were scratched on the grindstone and the bed-leg was sawed in two.

We were all pretty tired, especially Jim. And time was running out. Nobody had claimed Jim, so Uncle Silas was going to put a notice in the newspapers.

'It's time for the nonnamous letters,' Tom said.

'What's them?' I asked him.

'To warn Aunt Sally and Uncle Silas that something's wrong,' he replied. 'Otherwise, there'll be nobody to stop us and it won't be no fun!' He looked at me. 'You'll be the servant-girl that brings it.' He paused. 'And in the books, the prisoner always changes clothes with his mother and sneaks out that way. I'll be Jim's mother, Huck. I'll borrow a gown from Aunt Sally.'

'How will *you* get away, Tom?' I asked.

'I'll wear the servant-girl's frock you've got to borrow,' he said. He smiled at the thought of it. 'There's no time to lose, Huck!'

The next night, dressed in the servant girl's frock, I pushed this note under the front door:

Beware! Trouble is brewing. Keep a sharp lookout.
UNKNOWN FRIEND

Everybody was in a sweat and they put servants to guard the back and the front doors.

'Now for the best part of my plan!' Tom said.

He wrote:

There's a gang of cutthroats going to steal your slave at midnight

UNKNOWN FRIEND

Then he slipped down the lightning rod and stuck the letter in the collar of the sleeping guard.

We went fishing all day and found everybody in a terrible state when we came in for supper. We smuggled some food up to bed and Tom put on Aunt Sally's dress.

'Where's the butter?' Tom asked. 'Just you get down to the cellar and bring me some. I'll go and stuff Jim's clothes with straw. We'll run as soon as you get there.'

On my way from the cellar, Aunt Sally appeared at the top of the stairs. I hid the butter inside the hat on my head. She marched me angrily into the front room. My, there was a crowd there! Fifteen farmers, and each one holding a gun. Well, it got hotter and hotter and the butter came trickling down my forehead. Aunt Sally turned pale.

'Why, this child's brains are oozing out!' she cried.

She snatched off my hat and out comes what's left of the butter. And she was so pleased that I wasn't ill that she hugged me and sent me back to bed.

In a second, I was down the lightning rod and running to the cabin.

'Run, Tom!' I cried. 'There's fifteen men coming with guns.'

Chapter Ten

A good adventure

Tom's eyes blazed with excitement.

'Hurry! Hurry!' I shouted.

We heard footsteps outside the cabin door. Then in came some of the men, but they couldn't see us in the dark. We crawled outside and made for the fence in injun file.

'Who's there?' a man called out. 'Answer, or I'll shoot!'

We didn't answer. As the bullets whizzed around us, we ran to the canoe and paddled to the island where I'd hidden the raft.

'Now, old Jim,' I said, 'you're a free man again.'

'En a mighty good rescue it wuz, too, Huck,' Jim said. 'You planned it beautiful.'

'Boys, we did it!' Tom shouted.

Then we saw that Tom had a bullet in his leg.

'Don't stop now!' he begged. 'Push off, Jim!'

But Jim shook his head. He told me to take the canoe and fetch a doctor.

The doctor was a kind old man, but he complained that my canoe wasn't big enough for the two of us. He went to the island without me. As I waited for him to come back, I fell asleep and it was morning when I woke up. I ran to the doctor's house, but he wasn't there. When I was on my way to borrow a canoe, I bumped into Uncle Silas.

'Why, Tom!' he cried. 'Where have you been, you rascal?'

'I hain't been nowhere,' I said, 'only hunting that slave with Sid. We've bin paddling up and down the river all night.'

Aunt Sally was mighty glad to see me. She laughed and cried and hugged me and asked me where Sid was.

'Boys will be boys,' Uncle Silas said. 'He'll turn up.'

The next morning, as Aunt Sally looked out of the window, she shouted in surprise. Coming through the gate was Tom Sawyer on a mattress, the doctor and Jim wearing a dress, with his hands tied behind his back.

'Oh, Sid's dead!' she cried, running outside.

Tom turned his head towards her and she kissed him. Poor old Jim! The men locked him in the cabin again, and chained his hands and feet.

'Don't be rough on him,' the doctor said. 'He ain't a bad man. He helped me cut out the bullet.'

Tom was a lot better the next morning. As Aunt Sally and I sat by his bed, he opened his eyes.

'Huck, did you tell Aunt Sally?' he whispered. 'How we set the runaway slave free?'

'Dear, dear, the poor child's mad!' Aunt Sally said.

'No, I ain't,' Tom said. 'Me and Tom set him free. It took weeks of work, stealing candles and a shirt and no end of things. We done it all by ourselves.'

'Well, I never heard the likes of it!' Aunt Sally said. 'When you gets well, I'll… and don't you go meddling with Jim again.'

'Hasn't he got away?' Tom asked.

'They've got him back safe and sound in that cabin again,' Aunt Sally said. 'All chained up.'

Tom sat up, his face angry. 'They ain't got no *right* to lock him up!' he whispered. 'Turn him loose! His owner died two months ago. She set him free in her will.'

'Then why did you want to set him free if he was free?' Aunt Sally asked.

'Well, that's a good question,' Tom replied. 'I wanted

the adventure of it.' Suddenly, he stared at the doorway in amazement. 'Why, it's my Aunt Polly!' he cried.

Aunt Sally jumped up and hugged her sister, Polly. 'Tom never told me you was coming,' she said.

Aunt Polly looked at Tom over her spectacles. 'Tom!' she shouted. 'Why…?'

'That ain't Tom, it's Sid,' her sister said. 'But *where* is Tom?'

'Come out from under that bed, Huck Finn!' Aunt Polly cried.

We laughed and talked all that day. And Aunt Polly told us that Tom was right about Miss Watson setting Jim free in her will. So Tom Sawyer *had* gone to all that trouble – for nothing but an adventure.

Tom's well now and wears his bullet around his neck. 'One day,' he says, 'Let's all three go for an adventure.'

'Suits me,' I says. 'Likely my pap's got all my money from Judge Thatcher now. There ain't no use in me goin' back.'

'Your pap ain't comin' back no more, Huck,' Jim says sadly.

'Why not, Jim?' I ask.

And then he told me it was my pap dead in that floating house.

Now I reckon I got to get away 'cos Aunt Sally wants to adopt me and civilise me – and I can't stand it.

Yours truly, **HUCK FINN**

us that Tom was right about Miss Watson setting Jim free in her will. So Tom Sawyer *had* gone to all that trouble – for nothing but an adventure.

Tom's well now and wears his bullet around his neck. 'One day,' he says, 'Let's all three go for an adventure.'

'Suits me,' I says. 'Likely my pap's got all my money from Judge Thatcher now. There ain't no use in me goin' back.'

'Your pap ain't comin' back no more, Huck,' Jim says sadly.

'Why not, Jim?' I ask.

And then he told me it was my pap dead in that floating house.

Now I reckon I got to get away 'cos Aunt Sally wants to adopt me and civilise me – and I can't stand it.

Yours truly, **HUCK FINN**

Glossary

ambush 21
to launch a surprise attack

cabin 9, 14, 41, 42, 43, 45, 46, 47, 48
a room on a ship

cannon 10
a large and heavy gun

canoe 9, 10, 12, 13, 17, 18, 19, 22, 33, 35, 38, 41, 46, 47
a narrow boat, moved through the water with paddles

cellar 29, 45
a room in the basement of a house

civilize 7, 49
to educate and refine a previously-wild person

current 14, 17, 19, 22
flowing water

dawn 12, 13, 31, 41
the time of day when the sun rises

dazzling 29
brilliant

'didn't turn a hair' 33
'showed no reaction at all'

drag (a river) 9
to pull nets or hooks through a river
in search of someone or something

dusk 12, 19
the period during which day turns to night

enamel 23
the hard substance that teeth are made of

'everyone broke down' 29
'everyone started crying'

fire questions (at) 24
to bombard someone with questions

frauds 30, 33, 34, 35
dishonest people, tricksters

glimpse 11, 14
to catch sight of

grindstone 43
a disk-shaped stone used for sharpening metal

hare-lip 29
a condition some people are born with, by which they have a cleft in the middle of their top lip

hired 26
rented

'Honest injun, you ain't no ghost?' 39
'Do you promise you're not a ghost?'

'I hain't got no money, pap' 8
'I haven't got any money, dad'

'I'm a goner now' 22
'I'm going to be killed now'

'It's as mild as goose milk! 41
'It's too weak, it's not strong enough.'

'It's time for the nonnamous letters' 44

'It's time to send some anonymous letters.'

'keep people off your back' 24

'keep people away from you and stop them bothering you'

lantern 14, 16, 19

a type of portable light

laughing-stock 26

someone that everyone finds ridiculous or laughs at

lightning rod 40, 42, 45

a metal strip attached to a roof to draw lightning away from the rest of the building

meddle 48

to interfere

mosquitoes 22

iting insects

parlour 29, 31

a room mainly used for the reception of visitors

pelt (with) 27

to throw things at someone

play truant 7

to stay away from school without permission

pound 11

to thump

quarrelling 14, 20

arguing

raft 4, 11, 13, 14, 15, 16, 17, 18, 21, 22, 24, 25, 26, 27, 35, 36, 38, 41, 46

a flat vessel for transportation on water

resign 7

to leave a job or a club

rightful 23

correct and proper, by right

rouse 13

to wake someone up

run 11, 13, 14, 21, 22, 23, 24, 25, 26, 27, 45
to travel, sail

scoundrels 23, 26, 30, 32
bad people

skiff 15, 16, 18, 35
a small, light boat

slave trader 11
someone who bought and sold people as slaves

'slept the sleep of the dead' 16
slept really soundly

smallpox 18
an infectious illness

'struck out for the shore' 20
began to swim towards the shore

swamps 21
marshy areas

'tarred and feathered' 32

covered first in a layer of sticky tar and then in feathers as a form of punishment

tip-toe 11

to walk on your toes, making as little noise as possible

'turn (him) loose' 48

'set (him) free'

wade 22

to walk through water

watchman 16

a person who keeps watch

wigwam 14, 25, 38

a type of tent